ALLEN COUNTY PUBLIC LIBRARY

3 1833 03783 7955

**FRIENDS
OF ACPL**

HOLIDAY COLLECTION

O9-BTO-281

BEAR NOEL

Olivier Dunrea

FARRAR, STRAUS AND GIROUX • NEW YORK

Allen County Public Library
900 Webster Street
PO Box 2270
Fort Wayne, IN 46801-2270

Copyright © 2000 by Olivier Dunrea
All rights reserved
Distributed in Canada by Douglas & McIntyre Ltd.
Color separations by Hong Kong Scanner Arts
Printed and bound in the United States of America by Berryville Graphics
First edition, 2000

Library of Congress Cataloging-in-Publication Data
Dunrea, Olivier.
    Bear Noel / Olivier Dunrea. — 1st ed.
        p.   cm.
    Summary: The animals of the north woods react with excitement as they hear
Bear Noel coming to bring them Christmas.
    ISBN 0-374-39990-5
    [1. Bears—Fiction. 2. Animals—Fiction. 3. Christmas—Fiction.] I. Title.
PZ7.D922Be   2000
[E]—dc21   99-27600

For Kelly,
whose magnificent Bear Noels inspired this book

It is Christmas Eve in the north woods. Snow glistens white against a darkening sky. It shimmers and sparkles on the trees. Snow blankets the forest. It lies hushed and silent on the frozen ground.

In the quiet night, Bear Noel wends his way through deep white drifts, his heavy sack slung over one shoulder. This is the night when Bear Noel brings Christmas to the animals of the north woods.

Hare peeks from beneath snow-laden branches. Wolf lopes toward him. Wolf and Hare stare at each other.

"He is coming," whispers Hare.

"Who is coming?" Wolf asks.

"Bear Noel!" Hare cries.

In the distance they hear the thump of heavy footfalls in the forest.

Fox tilts her head and sniffs the night air. Across the snow, she sees Wolf and Hare dashing toward her.

"He is tramping through the snow," howls Wolf.

"He is coming," whispers Hare.

"Who is coming?" Fox asks.

"Bear Noel!" they cry.

They hear the merry jingle of bells.

Boar lifts his head and paws the snow. He snorts and stamps when he sees three figures charging toward him.

"He is jingling his bells," sings Fox.

"He is tramping through the snow," howls Wolf.

3 1833 03783 7959

"He is coming," whispers Hare.

"Who is coming?" asks Boar.

"Bear Noel!" they cry.

Through the forest they hear merry laughter.

Hedgehog creeps from her hole beneath the rocks.

She stares at the four rollicking animals.

"He is laughing," grunts Boar.

"He is jingling his bells," sings Fox.

"He is tramping through the snow," howls Wolf.

"He is coming," whispers Hare.

"Who is coming?" Hedgehog asks.

"Bear Noel!" they cry.

They hear joyful singing ringing through the woods.

Possum peers down from the branch of a tree. She curls her lips
and smiles as she watches five animals scampering across the snow.

"He is singing," pipes Hedgehog.

"He is laughing," grunts Boar.

"He is jingling his bells," sings Fox.

"He is tramping through the snow," howls Wolf.

"He is coming," whispers Hare.

"Who is coming?" Possum asks.

"Bear Noel!" they cry.

They hear jingling bells and laughter coming closer.

Owl swoops softly among the trees. Below, he sees six animals rolling and romping in the snow.

"He is getting nearer," purrs Possum.

"He is singing," pipes Hedgehog.

"He is laughing," grunts Boar.

"He is jingling his bells," sings Fox.

"He is tramping through the snow," howls Wolf.

"He is coming," whispers Hare.
"Who is coming?" Owl asks.
"Bear Noel!" they cry.
Nearby, a large white bear tramps through the snow.

Mole hears the sound of many feet rumbling over the snow.
He scrabbles up from his hole.

"He is bringing something wonderful," hoots Owl.

"He is getting nearer," purrs Possum.

"He is singing," pipes Hedgehog.

"He is laughing," grunts Boar.

"He is jingling his bells," sings Fox.

"He is tramping through the snow," howls Wolf.

"He is coming," whispers Hare.
"Who is coming?" Mole asks.
"Bear Noel!" they cry.

Into the clearing strides Bear Noel. His great furry feet sweep a broad
path through the snow. His bells jingle merrily.
Bear Noel tosses back his head and laughs.

The animals of the north woods tremble with excitement. They pause
and wait and hope.

Bear Noel stops by a small fir tree standing alone in the clearing.
He drops his heavy sack onto the snow. Hare and Wolf, Fox and
Boar, Hedgehog and Possum, Owl and Mole watch as Bear Noel
unpacks their gifts.

One by one Bear Noel hangs clusters of nuts and seed balls from the branches. He strings strands of bright red berries. Shimmering balls of sugar and salt sparkle among the green.

Bear Noel steps back and flings his arms wide. "Christmas is here!" he shouts. "Come gather round and feast. This is the night when all creatures may come together without fear."

For a brief moment the snow stops falling.

A bright star shines above the treetops. It is Christmas Eve in the north woods.

Bear Noel tramps slowly through the snow, his bells faintly ringing in the quiet night.